For Mom & Dad !

Tundra Books, an imprint of Penguin Random House Canada Young Readers,
a Penguin Random House Company

Library and Archives Canada Cataloguing in Publication

Title: Vote for me! / Ben Clanton.
Names: Clanton, Ben, 1988- author.
Identifiers: Canadiana (print) 20190088427 | Canadiana (ebook) 20190088435 |
ISBN 9780735267589 (hardcover) | ISBN 9780735267596 (EPUB)
Classification: LCC PZ7.C523 Vo 2020 | DDC j813/.6—dc23

Published simultaneously in the United States of America by Tundra Books of Northern New York,
an imprint of Penguin Random House Canada Young Readers, a Penguin Random House Company

Originally published in 2012 by Kids Can Press

Library of Congress Control Number: 2019937675

Edited by Tara Walker
Designed by Ben Clanton and Rachel Di Salle
The artwork in this book was rendered with pencil, watercolor, copy paper,
elephant poop paper and digital magic.
The text was set in Rockwell, Mrs Ant and Mr Dodo.

Printed and bound in China

www.penguinrandomhouse.ca

1   2   3   4   5   24   23   22   21   20

Penguin
Random House
TUNDRA BOOKS

* In fact, 97% of sheep agree that Donkey is #1.

Shoop!

BOOGER-BREATH!

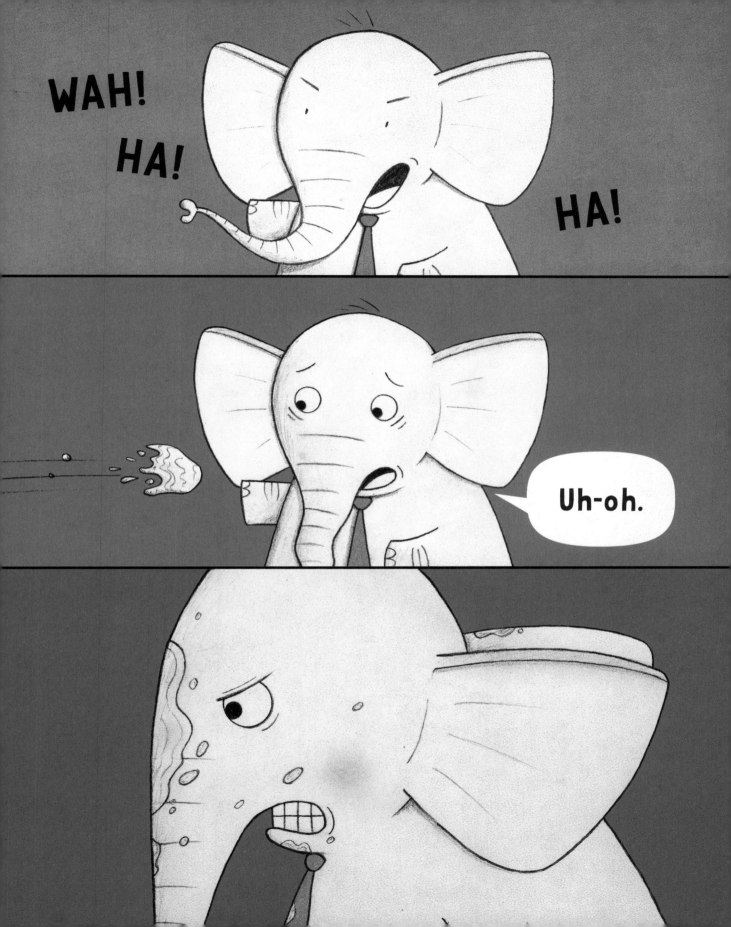

DUM

DONK

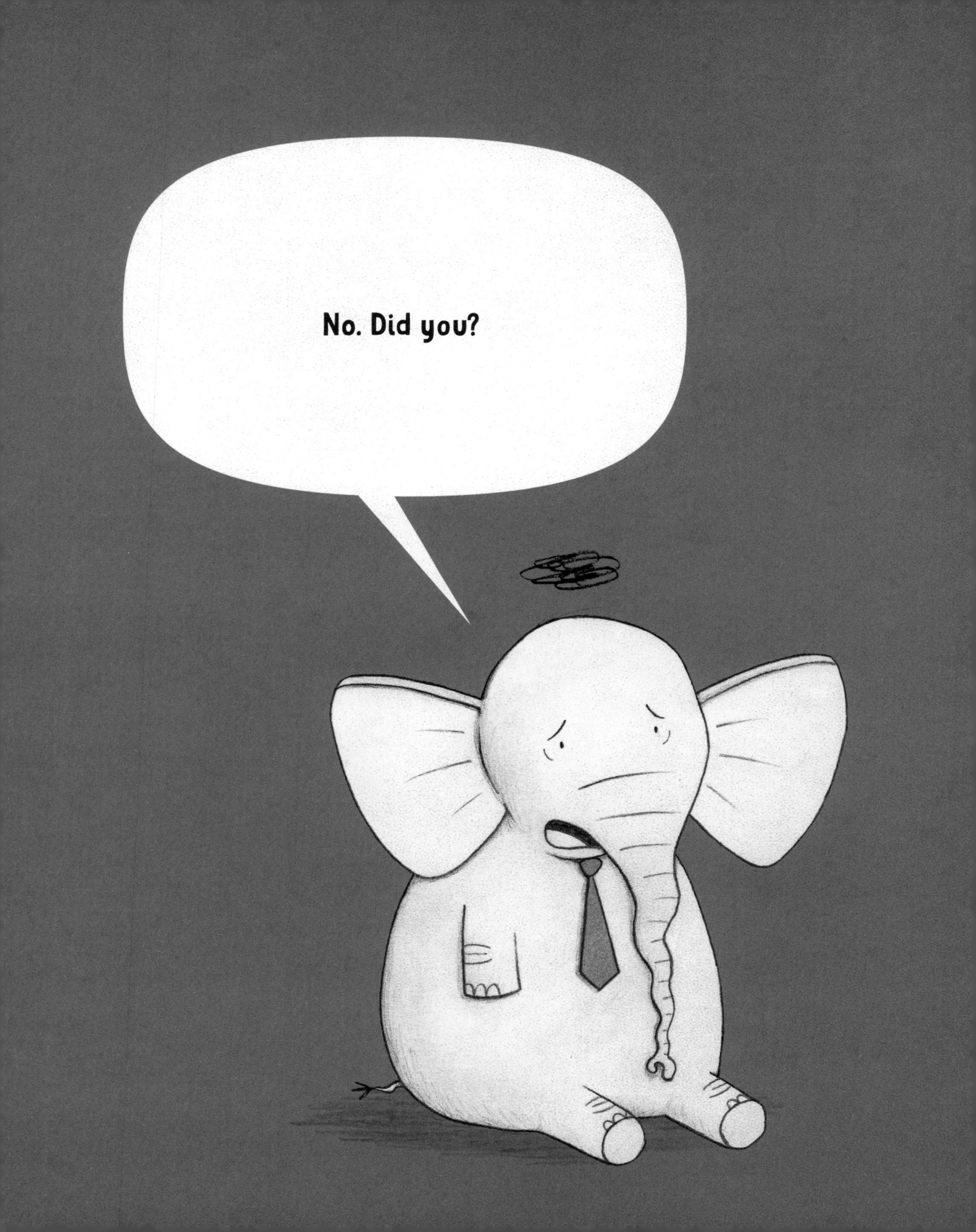
No. Did you?

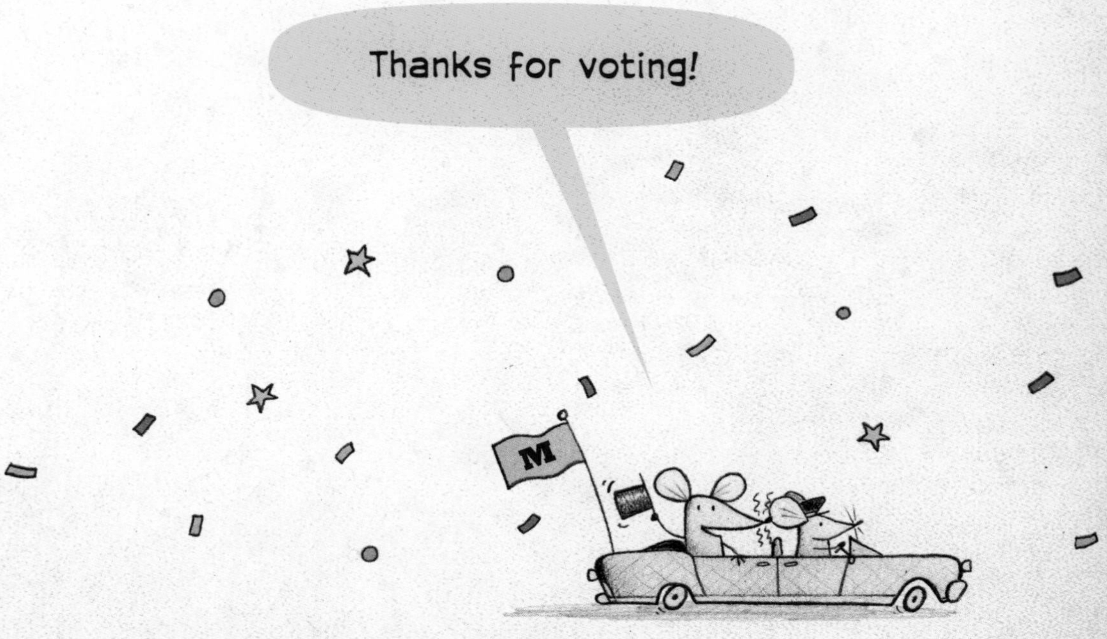
Thanks for voting!
M

NUH-UH
infinity and one.

Well, YUH-HUH
one more than whatever you say next
and there is nothing more, so that is

THE END.